P9-CRT-702

To Karen Morris, the librarian from
Stockton Libraries who inspired this story – J.J.

In memory of my mum – S.V.

American edition published in 2015 by Andersen Press USA,
an imprint of Andersen Press Ltd.
www.andersenpressusa.com
First published in Great Britain in 2015 by Andersen Press Ltd., 20 Vauxhall Bridge Road, London SW1V 2SA.
Published in Australia by Random House Australia Pty., Level 3, 100 Pacific Highway, North Sydney, NSW 2060.
Text copyright © Julia Jarman, 2015.
Illustration copyright © Susan Varley, 2015.

Distributed in the United States and Canada by
Lerner Publishing Group, Inc.
241 First Avenue North
Minneapolis, MN 55401 USA
For reading levels and more information, look up this title at www.lernerbooks.com.
Color separated in Switzerland by Photolitho AG, Zürich.
Printed and bound in Malaysia by Tien Wah Press.
Library of Congress Cataloging-in-Publication Data Available.
ISBN: 978-1-4677-9310-0
1-TWP-7/15/15

LOVELY OLD LION

JULIA JARMAN

SUSAN VARLEY

ANDERSEN PRESS USA

King Lion was Lenny's grandpa.
He was kind and clever but one afternoon,
when they were playing Snakes and Ladders,
he forgot the up and down rule.
And he couldn't remember Lenny's name.

Grandpa used to look proud and kingly,
but now he looked worried and tired.
One day he stared at Lenny's soccer ball.
He said, "What's that?" and he wouldn't
come outside for a game.

Another morning, Lenny
found his grandpa's crown
in the trash bin with some
other things that shouldn't
have been there.

King Lion kept getting muddled.
He even mixed up night and day.
He would say, "Goodnight, er... cub,"
and get into bed when the sun
was shining!

Grandma said, "Don't worry, Lenny. I'll play
with you. Grandpa's not himself today."
"Who is he then?" asked Lenny.
King Lion was still Grandpa!
But not so clever now, not so kingly,
and sometimes not so kind.

The other animals started to notice.
Once, when King Lion was singing
the same song over and over again,
Chimp laughed at him.
King Lion looked upset.
"Don't be mean!" Lenny
roared at Chimp.

Later, Hippo tried to explain
why King Lion was behaving oddly.
"He's getting old," he said, "and bits of him are
wearing out. His brain isn't working as well as
it did. That's why he keeps forgetting things."
"Then we must help him," said Lenny.
"And I know how!"

The next day, when they all met at
Lion's house, Lenny brought
his marble collection.
"It was Grandpa's," he said,
"when he was a cub."
King Lion's eyes
flickered when he
heard the marbles
rattle and he picked
up a shiny red and
white one.

"A red swirly," he said. "I beat Wildebeest with that one.
We were good mates when I was a cub."
"We still are," said Wildebeest. "Remember when we
played that trick on Croc?"

King Lion looked up.

"Did we hide his cherry bun?"

"He looked everywhere for it," laughed Wildebeest.

"And I found it," snapped Crocodile.

"With a bit of help from me," crowed Cockatoo.

The next day Wildebeest brought some photos with him.
"Remember that?" he said, pointing to one of Hippo in the bath.
"He was stuck," said King Lion, "but we pulled him out
and – SPLASH – we all got wet!" Grandpa laughed.

Lenny
and his friends kept
coming to see King Lion.
It cheered him up, but they
couldn't stop his tired old brain
from wearing out. As time passed
he got even more muddled.

One summer evening when Lenny found his
grandpa's crown in the grass, the old lion put
it on Lenny's head with his trembly paws.
"You will be King one day,"
he said, kindly.

Now Lenny *is* king and he has a son of his own.
King Lenny is kind and clever just like his grandpa was.
He sometimes forgets things now, but he never forgets
his grandpa. He often reminds the young animals in his
kingdom to be kind to their grandpas and grandmas,
and to help them to remember.